The Adventures of Duke and Dolly

Collie dog Duke and Indian runner duck Dolly are close friends. Dolly is amazed by all of Duke's canine senses, especially when he uses them to help others. Then it isn't long before Dolly realises she has her own special qualities . . .

In the next book in the series, *The Adventures of Duke and Dolly – The First Steps*, Duke and Dolly are joined by Ewe, a wise old sheep. Soon the courageous threesome set out to explore the bigger world, learning life lessons and finding out more about themselves, as they start to travel the globe.

Editorial: Ilsa Hawtin

Illustrator: Sonia Martinez

Design: Helen Nelson

THE ADVENTURES OF DUKE & DOLLY

BY CHANTAL BARNES

"Duke," asked Dolly,
"why do you sniff everything?"

"My sense of smell helps
me understand the world
around me," Duke replied.

Dolly looked puzzled –
how could sniffing things
help Duke understand
the world?

"Let me show you. Walk with me around the showground," said Duke.

"What can you smell, Dolly?" asked Duke.

Dolly sniffed the air.

"Burgers, hot dogs and chips," replied Dolly.

"Well, I can smell loads more than that, and with all the finer details. I can identify who was here, what they had to eat and how they were feeling.

"For example, I can detect the scent of a mother and child who passed by here, and I can even smell the fruit smoothie they drank."

"Wow. That's amazing," Dolly said in awe.

"Duke," asked Dolly, "why do you have such large ears?"

"My sense of hearing helps me understand the world around me."

"But I thought you said your nose did that?" Dolly looked perplexed.

"Walk with me towards the main arena," Duke replied.

"What can you hear?" asked Duke.

Dolly tilted her head to the side and then spun around in a complete circle.

"I can hear the music over the loudspeakers and the sound of horses' hooves," Dolly said.

Duke angled his ears back and forth, closed his eyes and remained absolutely still.

"Yes, there are horses and music," Duke began, "but there are many more sounds in the air. I can even hear the faint calls of a mother searching for her child."

"Wow. That's amazing. I can't hear that!" Dolly exclaimed.

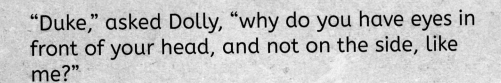

"Duke," asked Dolly, "why do you have eyes in front of your head, and not on the side, like me?"

"My sense of sight helps me understand the world around me," Duke replied.

Again, Dolly was puzzled.

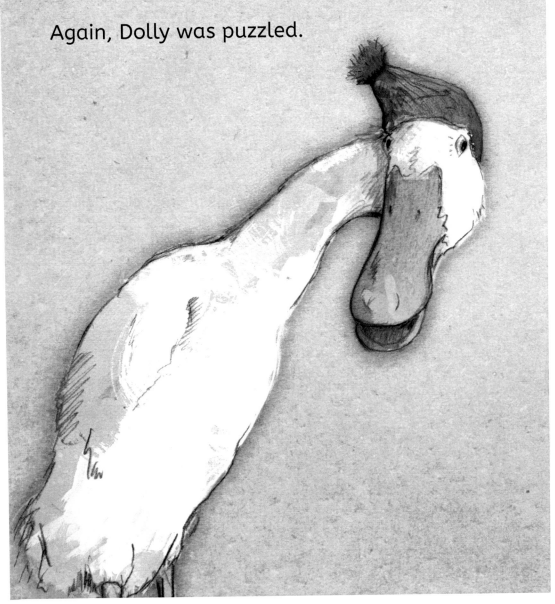

"Come into the marquee and I will show you,"
smiled Duke.

"What do you see?" Duke asked, after they had entered the large tent.

Dolly spun around quickly. "I see a table and you, Duke," replied Dolly.

"You are exactly right, Dolly," Duke replied, smiling, "but there's a whole lot more here.

With eyes on the front of my head, I am able to see depth and objects in the distance. Wait here a moment."

Duke walked over to the corner of the marquee.

When he returned, Dolly noticed a small child hanging onto his collar. The child looked upset.

"This young boy is lost," Duke said.

"I spotted him hiding in the corner on his own. He needs our help."

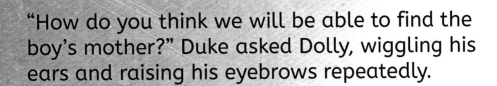

"How do you think we will be able to find the boy's mother?" Duke asked Dolly, wiggling his ears and raising his eyebrows repeatedly.

"I know – your senses! Let's use your senses!" laughed Dolly, walking with Duke and the child out into the open air.

"That's right, Dolly. I am going to smell with my nose, listen with my ears and look with my eyes."

And that's just what Duke did.

Dolly waddled beside Duke as he led the scared child around the showground.

Out of the corner of her eye, she watched as Duke tracked a scent, keeping his nose low to the ground as he moved forward with purpose, every now and again raising his eyes or turning his ears to pick up clues.

It wasn't long before Duke found the distraught mother and, with a relieved grin, the little boy let go of Duke's collar and leapt into his mother's welcoming arms.

Tears of joy rolled down both sets of cheeks, as they turned to Duke with gratitude for their reunion.

Duke and Dolly went along their way.

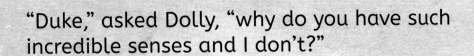

"Duke," asked Dolly, "why do you have such incredible senses and I don't?"

"We are two different species, you and I," replied Duke. "We each have our own traits that make us special."

Dolly sighed. "I'm not special," she said sadly. "I don't have senses like you, Duke."

"No, you don't have senses like me, but that's because you are built differently.

"You are an Indian runner duck, built to live in or around water, so you have many unique features that help you in that type of environment," explained Duke.

"I do? Like what?"
asked Dolly excitedly.

"Did your skin get wet when the rain fell earlier? Or when you swam on the pond?"

"No. My feathers make me waterproof," Dolly replied simply.

"Well, that's really incredible," Duke replied.

"And you can do something even more impressive than that, Dolly," Duke continued.

"I can? Like what?" asked Dolly, her eyes opened wide in excitement.

"You can float on water. This is a very special skill, Dolly, one that I wish I had," said Duke.

"You are right, Duke. I am special. Just like you," Dolly said in wonder.

Duke smiled.

It was a good day.

Made in the USA
San Bernardino, CA
20 January 2018